LEGS

The Story of a Giraffe

LEGS

The Story of a Giraffe

Phyllis Barber
illustrated by Ann Baumann

MARGARET K. MCELDERRY BOOKS
NEW YORK
MAXWELL MACMILLAN CANADA
TORONTO
MAXWELL MACMILLAN INTERNATIONAL PUBLISHING GROUP
NEW YORK OXFORD SINGAPORE SYDNEY

Margaret K. McElderry Books
Macmillan Publishing Company
866 Third Avenue
New York, NY 10022

Maxwell Macmillan Canada, Inc.
1200 Eglinton Avenue East
Suite 200
Don Mills, Ontario M3C 3N1

First edition
Printed and bound in the United States of America
Designed by Nancy B. Williams
1 2 3 4 5 6 7 8 9 10

Library of Congress Cataloging-in-Publication Data
Barber, Phyllis, date
Legs : the story of a giraffe / by Phyllis Barber ; illustrations
by Ann Baumann. —1st ed.
p.   cm.
Summary: A young giraffe growing up in Kenya is captured and
transported to a zoo.
ISBN 0-689-50526-4
1. Giraffes—Juvenile fiction.   [1. Giraffes—Fiction. 2. Zoo
animals—Fiction.]   I. Baumann, Ann, ill. II. Title.
PZ10.3.B232Le   1991
[Fic]—dc20   90-47679

To my father, the storyteller,
Herman Evans Nelson
—P. B.

For my loves:
Ben, Jacob, and Bob
—A. B.

Acknowledgments

Thanks to Agoi Hosking, storyteller and driver for Kenya Wildlife Travel; Anwar Hussein, tour director; LaMar Farnsworth, director of the Hogle Zoo in Salt Lake City, Utah; Marilyn Smoot, animal keeper at the Hogle Zoo; two authoritative texts, A Natural History of Giraffes *by Dorcas MacClintock and* The Book of the Giraffe *by C. A. Spinage; and special thanks to Paula Merwin.*

"The admirablest and fairest beast that I ever saw was a Jarraf."

—John Sanderson, a London merchant
who saw a giraffe at Constantinople in the year 1638

In 1414, the King of Bengal received a giraffe as a gift from East Africa. The Chinese ambassador in the King's court showed such interest in the animal that the King gave it to him for Emperor Cheng Tsu, third emperor of the Ming Dynasty. The Chinese believed it to be the *kilin,* a mythical beast in Confucian ideology, the Emblem of Perfect Virtue, Perfect Government and Perfect Harmony in the Empire and the Universe.

—from The Book of the Giraffe
by Clive A. Spinage *

1

One evening, in the land of Kenya, clouds crowded across the horizon and the face of the setting sun. But a sudden wind blew holes in the clouds and sunlight shone through like two large eyes. This was the moment when Imburugutu, a giraffe, was born. His name meant "long neck and sticking-up ears."

Eight giraffe cows gathered in a circle around his mother. Like lookout towers, they stood very still, watching the tall grasses surrounding them. If the grasses bent to one side, a hungry lion might be prowling there. The cows were constant sentries, except for one important moment: the moment when Imburugutu unfolded into the world.

First his forelegs came out of his mother. Then his head, all wrapped in a silky sack of membrane. After the cows saw that the new arrival would be all right, they quickly turned again to watch the movement of the grass. They knew *simba* the lion liked a tender meal, one that didn't know how to fight back.

Because his mother stood up to give birth, as giraffe mothers do, Imburugutu fell a long way to the ground—a hard drop from the comforting dark womb. *Smack!* He fell to the dust. Fine sand puffed into clouds all around him, and Imburugutu wanted to follow it as it rose up. But he was entangled by strands of membrane. He struggled to free himself, one leg, his neck, the other legs. Finally, he lifted his head proudly into the warmth of the setting sun. He had arrived! He was alive!

His mother bent to lick his face, his nose, and his eyes, and then captured an ear in her mouth and began to suck it clean. After she had finished with the other ear, he nuzzled into her soft underside and then rested his head on his woolly back with its pale spots. *Lala salama,* he seemed to say, *good-night.* And he drifted off for a few minutes, a long sleep for a giraffe.

After he woke, his eyes were filled with the majesty of his mother standing above him, more beautiful than anything he'd ever seen, though he had not seen very much. He didn't want to stay on the ground when she was up so high. He wanted a place by her.

Almost as if pulled by a magic string, he leaned onto his four spindly legs and rose to his full height of six feet. No small baby, this Imburugutu. Then he took a few miraculous steps with his untried, stiltlike legs.

With the first few steps, he felt like a new king, and after a few more, he fancied himself a frisky dancer.

His mother followed his every move for the first few days, and after that, he tagged her everywhere she went, wanting to play, wanting to nurse. But one day it was time for Imburugutu to learn independence. His mother told him *Kwa heri*—that she'd be back in a few hours, that this good-bye was not for long. Watching her until her neck seemed as small as a twig reaching up into a faraway acacia tree, Imburugutu stayed behind with a group of calves.

An old auntie cow, with coarse hairs fringing her lips, was left in charge of the babies. Imburugutu resented the way she followed him, bumping his neck when he lowered it to nibble the brush. She meant him to be mindful of lions and of food that could block his windpipe, but he didn't want to be taught anything except by his mother, and especially not on this bright day with the blaring blue sky spreading wide over his head.

Trying to escape the auntie cow's bossy ways, he trotted to the water hole for a drink. But his neck couldn't bend far enough to reach the water. Slowly, he slid his forelegs apart, the best way he knew to get to the water. And there she was again, bumping him in the flank, telling him not to split his legs so wide. She knew about the rainy season, when water holes turned to bogs of chalky, slippery mud. If Imburugutu's legs slid too far apart, he would tear the long tendon that connected the muscle of his upper leg to his hoof. He'd never stand again. She'd seen it happen before.

Imburugutu wanted her to leave him alone and tried to tell her so. But his voice was no bigger than the mewling of a baby cat. She grunted at him, which surprised Imburugutu because giraffes didn't have voices like the other animals, being mostly quiet and keeping their thoughts to themselves. He tried to grunt back at her, but only squeaked. Then he ducked underneath her belly and escaped.

With three other calves, Imburugutu ran against the wind through scrubby grass, termite hills, and dust, curling their long tails over their backs to keep them from tangling with the brush. The two legs on each side of their bodies moved together and carried them like loping camels until Imburugutu skidded to a sudden stop. He not only saw a strange tree with yellow bark and a bending trunk, but also heard it calling to him with an eerie, whistling sound.

Curious, he left his friends and circled the tree as a gust of wind blew his tail from side to side. In between the tree's wispy leaves, long thorns poked out from the branches like a thousand warriors' spears. And in between the spiky thorns, Imburugutu found small black pods, wrinkled and drying. He nibbled to see if they were good to eat until, suddenly, an entire battalion of nasty ants swarmed over his nose. Imburugutu backed up and shook his head in every direction he could, the ants biting with their ferocious jaws and telling him to mind his own business. The small black pods were theirs, stay away, don't come back. Imburugutu shook his head harder and showered the air with black ants, some of them falling back into the branches, some of them flying with the wind.

Stunned by the ants' rude welcome and annoyed at the gusty wind, Imburugutu heard the sound again. The tree whistled, just as before, and mesmerized Imburugutu as if it were a snake charmer's flute. He ventured closer, though not close enough to encounter more ants, and saw that some of the pods were empty except for a few small seeds rattling and spinning inside. When the wind whisked through the ant-carved holes in the pods, it made the whistling sound. Imburugutu was enchanted.

Besides the music coming from the pods, there were thousands of tiny green leaves on this tree—the sight of which made Imburugutu quiver with pleasure. He had a weakness for any kind of leaf, but these looked especially succulent. Slowly, he slithered his tongue, like a cautious snake, around the sharp thorns. And before long, he was not only stripping off leaves and empty black pods, but grasping whole branches with his tongue the way a monkey does with its tail. Then he crushed them with his jaws and happily swallowed them.

Imburugutu sighed with pleasure. The fresh taste of leaves, the aromatic sap from the bark—he would never need to move from this spot to find happiness. But just then, he heard a strange mix of sounds behind him. He turned to see the auntie cow racing toward him, her neck pulled back high in warning. He turned his head farther around to see a lioness charging him, straight as an arrow, splitting the tall grass as she ran toward him like wildfire, her powerful legs stretching out in front of her, devouring the distance between her and Imburugutu. But the auntie cow was running toward Imburugutu, too. She and the lioness were coming together like two sides of a triangle, ready to intersect at the point where Imburugutu stood. Suddenly he knew he must run as fast as he'd ever run, sailing over the plains and barely letting his hooves touch the ground.

Behind his flying heels, the giraffe cow and the lioness collided, the cow kicking the big cat's side, her eyes, her jaws, the cat snarling, swiping at the cow's leg with her paw, leaving long lines of claw marks on the surface. But when the cat crouched and started to spring up onto the auntie cow's back, the cow suddenly pivoted and slammed the leaping cat with her powerful neck. Stunned, the cat fell on her back and rolled to her side, immobile, the wind knocked from her.

The auntie cow ran quickly after Imburugutu, and

because her legs were longer and stronger, she soon caught up with him. He was winded and anxious to stop, but the cow made him keep running until they reached the place where Imburugutu's mother was browsing peacefully. Before she left his side, however, the auntie cow fussed at him for running from the circle of her care. Then, with her nose, she pushed him toward his mother, who was waiting, her elegant shape outlined by the intensifying blue of the sky at sunset, a dark shadow of long neck and sticking-up ears. She pushed him back to his mother's soft underside with its fine dinner of mild milk, back to the safety of her feet as the night settled in, back to the shelter of his nest of grass.

As Imburugutu grew bigger, getting up from sitting down became an awkward thing to do. His mother began nudging him to his feet every time he sat down. Always and forever, she told him, he must be mindful of *simba.* But Imburugutu hadn't forgotten his day with the auntie cow. Except for the very young and very old giraffes, and for the dry times when *simba* could find no other food, Imburugutu knew firsthand that lions were very respectful of giraffes.

Actually, the animals that frightened Imburugutu most were the two-legged *wawindaji,* the hunters. All animals gave their lives to be somebody else's dinner or to the earth for renewal. The animals accepted this fact.

But the two-legged *wawindaji* often took more than they needed. They hunted the tusks of *tembo* the elephant and *kifaru* the rhinoceros and left the rest of the animal behind. They took the skins of *mamba* the crocodile, of *simba* the lion, and of *chui* the leopard. Imburugutu did not know that the hunters sold the skins to be made into shoes and purses, rugs and coats. Or that some of them wanted *twiga* the giraffe's spotted hide and the beautiful silken hair of its tail for making bracelets to sell. The hunters tried to catch the biggest giraffes with nets and ropes, but most of the time Imburugutu's long-legged elders ran much too fast from these hunters. Luckily, they hadn't tried to catch Imburugutu yet. He was still half-grown; his tail was scraggly; and his horns were just beginning to appear on top of his head.

One day when Imburugutu was sniffing out the best leaves in a treetop, he heard a roaring blast. All the giraffes instantly pulled their heads out of the trees and scattered. Imburugutu ran with them, but turned his head to see what had happened. There, underneath an umbrella acacia tree, his own mother had fallen into dust that whirled like fright. Two *wawindaji* were standing over her with smoking sticks on their shoulders. One bent to take her tail from her, then both ran to the high bushes.

Imburugutu moved in closer, but carefully. Maybe the hunters were watching him. He waited for his mother to get up, but she lay still, like a stone.

Above them, three shadows circled. Shadow and light drifted across his mother's body like waves of an ocean and created the illusion that she was moving. But then the shadows settled into hunchback forms that perched on the highest branches, stepping with one clawed foot and then the other. Imburugutu knew these vultures, the hovering birds as familiar to him as the whistling thorn had become. They were here for his mother. He slid his hoof slowly until it touched her curiously quiet body. His confused thoughts raced around and around until they formed a hardness in his neck where he swallowed. He bent his forelegs to lower himself and sniffed her special smell, which he knew so well. She didn't sniff him back. She didn't nudge him under the chin.

Kwa heri, he said with no words, *good-bye.* He struggled to stand, then stretched for some comforting acacia leaves. Crushing them slowly, he searched for something else to watch, something new for his eyes, because the picture of his mother wasn't a good one.

He saw a starling sitting in the treetop and eyeing him intently. The white band between the bird's purple neck and orange breast stretched wide as the bird began to warble. Its song was strong like a new sunrise. *You're not alone,* it seemed to be telling him, *not today, not tomorrow.* Then it flapped its jade-green wings and lifted up out of the acacia's thorns. *Don't forget,* it whistled.

The hardness in Imburugutu's neck softened. Bright drops of water slipped over the rim of his eyes and tracked across three brown patches on his cheeks. He watched the bird shimmer like a jewel as it rose into the air and was carried away by a current of air. He looked back at his own tail and thought of the times when it, too, sailed as he ran.

But then the sour odor of the black sticks the hunters had carried filled his nostrils. He could never forget that smell, or the sharp, cracking sound that had split the air into pieces and pounded against his ears. He'd run away like lightning if they came again. And yet, at the edge of these worries, he heard the starling calling out of the wide sky. *Don't forget. Don't forget.*

2

Imburugutu grew faster than the days came around. He looked forward to the time when he would be fully grown, maybe as high as the tallest acacia tree and as heavy as a thundercloud. Maybe, he sometimes imagined, he'd have a neck longer than the whole of his mother. Then he could show the other males who was boss, as the grown-up bulls did. They slammed each others' heads, rubbed necks, and twined them like a braid to see who was most powerful.

Sometimes Imburugutu sparred playfully with other calves, but just now, his neck was being used as a stairway by a pesky oxpecker with a red bill. Sometimes the bird ran up and down Imburugutu's neck; sometimes it glided backward from his ears clear down his leg. Imburugutu tried to shake this ash-brown pest from his neck. But then it settled back down like dust and traipsed over his face, hunting for ticks and blood-sucking flies. After days of annoying skirmishes, Imburugutu decided to let things be. He surrendered to this bird with yellow rings around its eyes. There were some advantages. He needed help with the ticks that burrowed in his hide. And he could take short cat-naps with the bird around. He could trust its red bill to sound an alarm if anything out of the ordinary came near.

And at that very moment, Imburugutu was startled out of his reverie by the oxpecker's hissing. *"Tsssss. Tsssss."* Closing in on both of them was a fast-moving truck with two dark silhouettes of *wawindaji* inside. Maybe they were the two hunters he'd seen before.

Imburugutu ran the way he had when he'd seen the lioness. His body rocked like a ship on the ocean as he took giant strides, double the height of a tall *wawindaji.* He galloped past sausage trees, a grove of acacias, and a herd of wildebeest. He galloped past whistling thorns with no temptation to stop, even though he heard the music spinning in the pods. But the truck covered with many spots of mud kept up with Imburugutu and forced him toward the river where Imburugutu would stop because he couldn't swim. He slowed to change his direction, but at that moment, he felt something slide over his head and down his neck. It felt like someone's tail, and it bit into his muscles. He twisted and bobbed his neck, but couldn't shake loose.

"Stop!" one of the men yelled. When the truck stopped, a cloud of dust covered the men and Imburugutu until they could barely see each other.

Imburugutu closed his nostrils to protect their inner linings, but the two *wawindaji* coughed and hacked before they could tend to the business of the stiff, coarse rope.

"Steady, *twiga*," they said. "Whoa, boy."

Imburugutu was very unhappy. No matter which way he moved, the rope stayed with him as if it were part of his body. He kicked and bucked and made a worse dust cloud than before. Then he swung his head with as much force as a young giraffe could muster and tried to slam the *wawindaji* into the side of the truck. The men were too quick, and jumped well out of reach.

"Tie the rope to the winch," one yelled to the other.

"He's a lively one," the other shouted, leaping into the back of the truck. "It's a good thing he's still a youngster." He looped the rope over the winch and cranked the handle as fast as he could. Imburugutu kicked and bucked, but the length of the rope grew shorter as he was pulled close to the body of the truck, like an anchor.

"Get on his back, mate. It's the only way."

The man on the truck bed took a running jump and threw himself onto Imburugutu, who twisted his neck to the left, then to the right, snapping at the *wawindaji.*

Imburugutu arched and jerked away from the nuisance on his back, more and more delirious with his fear of the smoking sticks. Instead of a booming sound and black smoke, however, he felt a firm hand stroking him and then prickling sensations traveling up his neck as something was lifted on a long pole to cover his head.

"This blanket'll calm you down, *bwana twiga*. We don't want to hurt you." The man patted Imburugutu's straw-brown paintbrush mane. "But how else could we catch you? You're so fast, beautiful *twiga*. Such soft, silky skin. And eyelashes like awnings on store windows."

"The blindfold worked, mate. He's calming some."

"Lower the tailgate ramp," said the other. "I can get him in the truck if we both move slowly." The man leaned against Imburugutu's neck and whispered up to his tall ears. "Yes, *twiga,* we're taking you to the world. People want to meet you, and they'll pay us for the privilege."

The hand felt warm as his mother's tongue once had, and the darkness over his eyes soothed his nervousness. Imburugutu's heart stopped pounding like an angry fist against his chest.

"Just a few steps." The man on his back still slid his soothing hand up and down Imburugutu's neck. "This rope is bad for your health, I know, so no more after this. I promise." Imburugutu had no other

choice but to follow the rope's pull. It burned his neck like a ring of fire. Up a slanting ramp and into a wooden crate with no top. There was a click of a latch. Imburugutu had no place to run now. The man on his back lifted the blanket, untied the rope from his neck, and climbed out over the walls of the crate.

The hunters disappeared into the cab of the truck, and the truck huffed and whined while Imburugutu butted against the sides of the crate. As the truck maneuvered around swampy patches of grass and deep ruts, he watched umbrella acacias and whistling thorns glide past. The odd thing was, they moved while his legs stood absolutely still. That had never happened before. Dust swirled around him in his wooden house. He blinked cautiously as a thick layer of brown powder settled on his eyelashes and sifted into his throat.

Suddenly he felt something pecking between one of his ears and one horn. It was his old friend, the oxpecker, foraging for parasites in his hide, the same red-billed pest. It tracked down to Imburugutu's eyes and looked into them curiously. Imburugutu looked back, his eyes large and black and shining with uncertainty, his legs shifting nervously with every bump.

The truck's round wheels couldn't step over the steep-sided ruts in the road as Imburugutu could, so they hit every rock and splashed into every water hole until Imburugutu felt sick inside.

As they rolled on, Imburugutu and the oxpecker

saw tall necks sticking up in the trees. There was the auntie cow, her head stretched gracefully into boughs of umbrella acacia. And there were lionesses nursing their babies while other cubs nipped at their father's tail. The father *simba* cuffed a cub with his paw and sent it running back to its mother. They saw *tembo* the elephant dig into the salt lick with his ivory tusks and roll a ball of mud into the cradle of his trunk. And they saw weaverbirds building nests with protected entrances away from the branches. There were Egyptian geese waddling along a riverbank, and always the vultures, shifting their weight in the treetops as they waited for the next meal. The familiar changed to the unfamiliar as Imburugutu, the oxpecker, and the truck wheels kept rolling.

Faithfully, the bird stayed with Imburugutu until the sun began to drop from the sky. Then it took one final glide down Imburugutu's neck, walked over his back to give him one last going over, and then hopped in between Imburugutu's horns where it teetered unsteadily, because of the bumping motion of the truck. It hissed a lingering farewell and flew back the way the truck had come, its black shadow stark against the pink and blue sky.

Imburugutu watched it fly into the last of the day. As it faded, he saw eyes of light shining through two partings in the clouds, something he'd seen before at sunset, something he hoped to see again. And he felt he was being watched as he traveled away from his home.

3

They bumped over dusty roads for two days and a night and passed through many *vijiji,* the villages where people lived, wove baskets, carved wooden figures, and sold their vegetables from blankets on the ground. Finally they arrived at the largest water hole Imburugutu had ever seen. It stretched away from him farther than he could imagine, and the waters seemed very restless.

"Time to part our ways, *bwana twiga,*" the *wawindaji* said as they tied ropes around the braces on the crate and hooked them to a wire cable.

When his wooden house was lifted high over the water and lowered to the deck of a freighter, Imburugutu's heart felt as if it were frantically trying to leap to dry land. Then Imburugutu saw bushbuck, cheetah, and zebra being lowered into a dark hole below the deck, and he panicked even more. He

strained against the sides of his crate to find a way out before he, too, ended up in the black hole. But instead of being dropped into darkness like the others, his crate was lashed to cables on the open deck by quick-moving men who muttered while they worked.

"Too tall for the hold. Grotesque." They laughed. "A freakish-looking camel." But Imburugutu didn't mind. His long neck had saved him from the black hole.

He was relieved when he heard the other animals complaining from below, even the baboon screeching. That meant they were alive, although their voices were almost overpowered by the sound of the creaking freighter and the choppy waves whipping its sides. But something, some magic, started happening around him.

The sun was sinking into the huge water hole, red and round like a wheel on the *wawindaji* truck. It seemed to be running away from the moon, which was popping up on the opposite side of the sky. The moon climbed as the sky changed from yellow to orange, then to red, purple, blue, and finally black. And it brightened and puffed out round and full. Then, to Imburugutu's surprise, he saw a long tail of light stretch across the black night water and spread wide like a fan. He had never known that the moon had a tail like that.

That night, even though Imburugutu was given damp, musty alfalfa to chew instead of the fresh leaves he loved, the tail of the moon, which reached out to him through the night, made him feel contented and safe.

But when the sun rose red the next morning, the magic disappeared. The sea grew rougher and the wind blew harder against his eyes than ever before. He saw a dark storm hang above the freighter. His legs filled with shaking, but he couldn't sit down inside the narrow walls of his crate. The boat swayed and rocked and leaned hard to one side and then the other. Wind and water stung his eyes.

Below, Imburugutu heard *punda milia* the zebra kicking the sides of his crate, the cheetah clawing at his wooden box, and the baboon screeching so loud that the noise hurt Imburugutu's sticking-up ears as much as the cutting rain hurt his face.

Water tumbled over the sides of the freighter, and strong winds pushed against Imburugutu's eyes and nose. The voices of all the animals tangled into one fearful harmony as rain pelted down on his head, his ears, and his neck. He had no tall branches to hide in for shelter as he stuck out of the top of his crate. His stomach was swimming. He was dizzy. His neck felt as stiff as a wooden board, and salt water spat at him over and over.

When he heard the zebra bucking and slashing at his own belly with his hooves, Imburugutu became more frightened. The rocking, shuddering, and lurch-

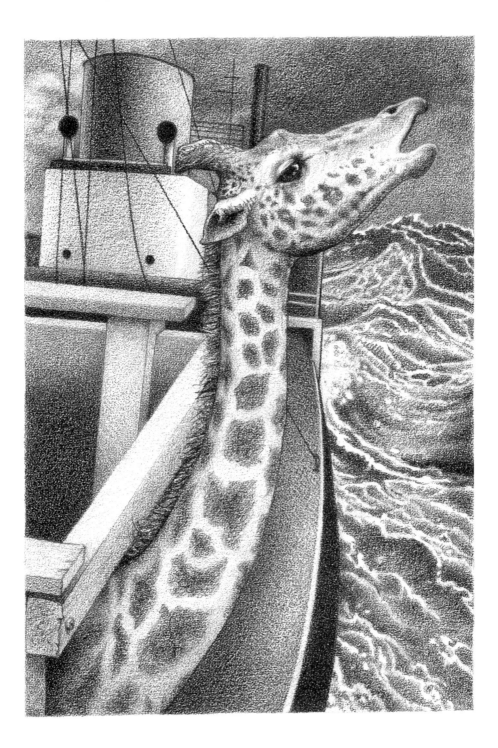

ing from side to side seemed greater than the big boat itself. Maybe it would fall to pieces, and the giant mouths between the waves would swallow the freighter and the crew and the animals. Maybe their time had come to be somebody else's dinner.

Imburugutu closed his eyes to protect them from his fears and from the stinging salt water. Inside the darkness of his eyelids, he conjured up a picture of the moon's tail from the night before—the shimmering rays breaking through night clouds, shooting light to Imburugutu's whistling thorn trees and spilling to the ground he'd walked on, far, far away from this great water hole.

The moon. The sun. He squeezed his eyes open to a small sliver of sight. There, as big as the tail of last night's moon, he saw a wide beam of sunlight. It was cutting through the heavy bank of clouds. First one eye in the clouds, then two, then the blazing face of the sun unveiled.

And gradually, Imburugutu and the sea relaxed to bask in the return of light.

4

A truck received the tall cargo from the freighter and, after winding through mountain passes and many towns where people stared at the top of Imburugutu in disbelief, it stopped at its destination: a large group of cinder-block buildings flanked by wire-fence pens.

"This is almost your home," a man said to Imburugutu as he unlatched the crate's gate. "You're in the holding pens just outside of the zoo until the vet gives you a clean bill of health. Then you'll move to the Giraffe House with the big boys."

Imburugutu was hesitant to leave the four walls to which he'd grown accustomed. But not far away there were massive trees with thousands of large, full-faced leaves. The wind blew slightly, rustling and shifting their shiny surfaces. The leaves mirrored pieces of sunlight and seemed to play a strange leaf music Imburugutu had never heard before.

"Come on, Mr. Giraffe," the man said, holding out a branch of the same succulent leaves. "You're safe here. Down this ramp. Come on."

Imburugutu didn't understand the idea of down. It was something he'd never done before. He assessed the slanting ramp, then stepped back and rested his neck on the edge of his tall crate.

"Hey, you! Mr. Giraffe." The man shook the branch.

After the salt-soaked alfalfa on the ship and the stale alfalfa on the truck, these fresh new leaves were irresistible. Their fragrance played at the tips of Imburugutu's nostrils and almost pulled him toward the ramp. Very slowly, he followed the leaves, taking each step as if there were eggs lying in his path and to be avoided. Carefully. Slowly. Until his hooves touched level ground.

"Move it!" the driver yelled. "I don't have all day." He revved the truck's engine. The man with the branch stretched up on his toes to give Imburugutu the promised gift of leaves. Then he jumped onto the rolling truck, which stopped only long enough for him to lock the gate.

Imburugutu watched black fumes spiraling out of the truck's rusty tailpipe as it roared away. He wasn't anywhere near the trees he'd been planning to browse on. He was in a cage of diamond-shaped wire. He was alone with a bundle of dried alfalfa stacked on a hard metal shelf. All he could do was stare over a high fence

and dream about crushing those fresh, crisp leaves between his jaws.

As the trees turned into silhouettes and blurred into evening shadow, Imburugutu paced more restlessly. He wished for his mother and his home. He wished for a way to the leafy trees. The cage was narrow and made the world seem big everywhere except where he was. As nervous as if a snake was coiled beneath his belly, Imburugutu feared what might surprise him out of the dark in this place where he couldn't run. He heard other animals speaking uncertainly into the night—the familiar voices of *nyani* the baboon and *fisi* the hyena, and new voices he'd never heard before. He heard many languages of fear, many new rhythms of animals circling in cages too small for them, too, and his world closed more tightly around him. Maybe the large mouth of the dark was hungry for him. He imagined lions snapping at his tail, snakes hissing under his belly, hunters with smoking sticks chasing him through the night. He banged against the sides of the fence. His legs, body, and neck trembled.

Then something inside warned him that his fear was growing too wildly. Cautiously, he looked to the sides, to the front and back of himself. Nothing was chasing him. No lions. No jaws. No fiery eyes glowing. He looked at his feet. No snakes. No sounds except for the leaves that whispered soothing songs to Imburugutu. Gradually, the black night softened and the sky

turned a pale and quivering pink. Imburugutu knew his old friend would soon show its eyes on the horizon. His friend who came out to shine on Imburugutu every day, no matter where he was. He watched the tip of the sun peek over the trees and then round out to a full circle. His most loyal friend! Maybe everything would be all right.

5

"What a beauty," the veterinarian said as he walked into the holding pen. He brushed the caked sea salt from Imburugutu's coat and examined his big eyes.

"He looks pretty healthy, but we'll have to see."

The inspector mumbled to himself as he wrote on his chart. "Blood tests every Thursday. Hoof-and-mouth tests tomorrow, with two follow-ups at two-week intervals. Rinderpest on Fridays. Check what else he might have brought from home."

Imburugutu stood alone most of the time, visited once a day by people in white jackets who poked strange instruments at him. They checked his coat for roughness, watching to see if the hair stood on end rather than lying flat against his body. They took samples of his blood. Imburugutu didn't like to see the white jackets come, but he did watch for the woman in a green uniform who drove the truck with bales of alfalfa in the back. She had one very long dark braid, which would nearly have touched the earth if she hadn't looped it back on itself. Her skin was like Imburugutu's patches—a bronze, sun-baked color, and she moved like a supple branch when she picked up the bales of alfalfa and tossed them onto Imburugutu's metal shelf.

The best thing about the woman in green was that she didn't poke him with anything. And she sometimes stopped to talk as she stood in the back of her truck.

"You'll be coming to live with me and the giraffes in a few weeks," she said to Imburugutu one day. "But I want to get to know you first. My grandfather, who was a medicine chief, told me to listen to the animals, to watch them carefully. If I did that, he said, flowers would open in my mind, and I would know answers."

Imburugutu looked at her placidly, yet held his head and neck a little higher than in the past few weeks. She made him feel like an entire tree growing straight out of the land as she looked into his eyes.

"My name is Onosa. One of these days, I'll give you a name, but I have to wait for the right one to come to me. Meanwhile, on a day when I finish delivering the alfalfa early, I'm going to sit and watch you. Just you. I want to know your particular secret."

Days began and days ended without Onosa keeping her promise. Sometimes a red ant would crawl along Imburugutu's fence, or a bird would light on the wire and jabber about something or other. Sometimes a mouse would crawl out of the alfalfa, squeak at Imburugutu, and then burrow back into the bale of leafy hay. With the exception of these few friends who never stayed long, the days seemed thin and pale in this place. Imburugutu had the strongest urge to feel his legs moving again: to run back to the great wide spaces where his elders rubbed necks, where he'd eaten bright yellow thorn blossoms with his friends, where he'd watched animals coming and going. Even though he now heard many voices floating in the air, there were no bodies for his eyes to see.

One day while Imburugutu was gazing once again at his favorite trees, Onosa came without her truck. She undid the loop in her braid and let it fall to the ground as she sat cross-legged outside his cage. She put her elbows on her knees and her fists under her chin and stared at Imburugutu.

"You're not in any hurry," she said. "And you are like a big mountain chief. Your eyes are high up like the eagle who flies. What do you see up there? Do you see the top of the whirlwind? Whatever you see, I think you seem happy enough with who you are. You aren't trying to be anybody else or any better than you already are. But how could you possibly be any better? You're already so beautiful."

Imburugutu wished she would not sit so far away from him. She stopped talking, so he started pacing again and looking longingly out at the trees.

"You're always wishing for trees," she said. She stood up, went over to the trees, and stripped a delicate branch from one of them.

"A bouquet of leaves," she said to Imburugutu.

Imburugutu bent his neck to rub the side of his face against the palm of her outstretched hand. Nothing made him happier than green leaves and friends who understood something about him.

"Your quarantine's almost over," she said, "and I can watch you even better at the Giraffe House. And maybe I'd better get back to work now. Here comes the inspector."

She put the toes of her boots into the fence, climbed up to Imburugutu's eye level, poked her fingers through the wire, and traced the line of his jaw. "Thank you," she said. "You can teach me more at the Giraffe House."

"Think this one's ready to join you, Onnie?" the inspector asked as he unlocked the gate and stepped inside.

"He's been ready since the day he came," she said. "A perfect giraffe."

"So, you're a perfect giraffe," the inspector said, rubbing Imburugutu's skin to check for texture one last time. "All right, Mr. Giraffe. You've passed inspection. You're healthy. No exotic new diseases and none of the old ones. You're A-OK, even perfect," he

said, winking at Onosa before he signed his name to a stack of papers.

"And you've grown at least a foot while you've been here. Used to be I could look at your neck at eye level. Pretty soon, I'll be looking at your knees. Better get him on his way before he's too big to transport."

The next morning, a forklift carrying an empty crate arrived alongside Onosa's feed truck.

"Set it on the ground," she shouted to the forklift operator as she jumped out of the truck. Then she walked over to the trees Imburugutu loved for another sheaf of its leaves. "Come on," she shouted as she ran back, shaking the leaves under his nose. Without hesitation, he passed through the pen's gate and followed her into the crate. "Good boy," she said, easing around him and out the gate, where she slid the bolt into place.

"Hope you don't get into trouble someday," she said. "You'll go anywhere for leaves!"

As the forklift raised Imburugutu's crate off the ground, he noticed how much he had grown. His neck stuck farther out of his crate than before. He was almost a tree himself, as his mother had seemed to him on the first day of his birth.

Onosa checked to see that the crate was secured, then ducked into the cab of her truck. She waved good-bye to the forklift operator. "See you over at the Giraffe House. I'm taking a shortcut."

The truck rolled out the gate. Imburugutu was on his way once again, rolling into something he'd never known before. But there were trees shading the path they followed, and the sun shone warm through the haze of autumn. Those things softened the sharp edges of the unknown.

6

"He's here. He's here."

People were packed shoulder to shoulder against a wire mesh fence. One of them, a lady in a yellow flowered dress with a yellow flowered handkerchief, waved at Imburugutu. The blossoms on the material reminded him of the succulent spring flowers on the whistling thorn, and his mouth watered. He was just about to reach over for a nibble of their tenderness, when dozens of flashbulbs exploded. His eyes filled with fiery suns. Even when he blinked, the suns persisted.

"Smile," a man with a camera said. "Say cheese." Somebody laughed. "He's a big one!" a little girl with a pinwheel lollipop said. Everyone seemed to be having a party as Imburugutu's cage was lowered to the ground and the gate on his crate was opened.

"You can come out now," he heard Onosa say, but

he was frightened by the noisy voices and flashing cameras and by the sunlight glinting off people's eyeglasses and the metal handles of baby strollers.

"It's safe here," she coaxed. "And you don't have to step down. Come with me and meet your Masai cousins. They're a bit different than you Baringo giraffes."

As usual, Imburugutu was tempted by a branch of leaves Onosa held in her hands. But as he inched out of his crate, taking mincing, hesitant steps, one of the two corrugated metal doors on the cinder-block building in front of him opened. It rumbled like thunder. Imburugutu panicked, ran past Onosa, and almost knocked her over.

"Whoa," she yelled, running after him and rattling the leaves. "Nothing's going to hurt you. Slow down!"

Leaves or no leaves, Imburugutu ran from the frightening thunder, but he couldn't run far enough. There was no wide expanse of flat land where he could pick up speed—just a triangle yard with a high rock wall on one side, a tall wire fence on the other, and the gray blocks of building behind him. So Imburugutu ran in circles. Onosa chased him. "Calm down. You're going to slip and fall. Whoa, boy!"

But suddenly, he saw something that did slow him. Three familiar faces on three familiar long necks arched out of the open door of the gray building. He stopped running and stared in amazement at their skin that was covered with patterns of dark jagged leaves. It was unlike his coat with its network of wide white lines. He hadn't seen another giraffe since he left the dusty plains of his home. And now there were three with very unusual skin! Instantly, Imburugutu forgot the thunder and trotted over to them, but the three giraffes pulled their heads back inside as if the building were a turtle shell and they were turtles. When Imburugutu peered inside, he saw them chewing nonchalantly on bunches of alfalfa and acting as if he wasn't there.

He was too curious to be hurt by their indifference, so he walked through the doorway for a closer look. The three giraffes were unlike any he'd ever seen. They had different-shaped patches on their hides, almost like leaves or zigzags of lightning he'd watched in the sky. But they still had long necks and sticking-up ears and looked very much like his friends from home.

Here I am, he wanted to say. *I've come a long way.*

The youngest of the two males in the group lowered his head to warn Imburugutu not to come any nearer.

When Imburugutu didn't move, the giraffe began swinging his neck in an arc, a sign of war. His message was clear.

Surprised, Imburugutu trotted back to the paddock. A few people snapped more pictures of him, but the crowd that had gathered to welcome him had thinned out. Onosa was waiting with her ever-ready branch of leaves.

"I thought that might happen when you met the others," she said as she gave him his treat. "But don't worry! It's only a matter of time. Meanwhile, I'll shut their door so they'll leave you alone."

Onosa disappeared while Imburugutu mashed leaves in his mouth. And then he heard the thunder again. But this time, he realized it was the door, not thunder with lightning hidden in its growl. No need to run from it! He sniffed the rocks in the high wall and explored the fence and railing with his tongue. And then he heard the sound of moving air and flapping wings.

Out of nowhere, a fluffy black guinea hen with white spots hopped up to the railing. It perched fat and full on the fence, looking down at Imburugutu with its black bead eyes.

"Ca-coo, ca-coo, tuk tuk tuk," she said in a friendly way.

Imburugutu was interested in the sound of her voice.

She cackled and sputtered until she almost lost her balance. Maybe she'd noticed how the other giraffes had treated Imburugutu. Maybe she was visiting to help ease his aloneness.

Imburugutu wanted to tell her how he'd had several bird friends in his home. About how a starling said he wasn't alone. About how he could go to sleep with the oxpecker on his neck and not worry about trouble. About how happy he was to meet someone friendly like her. But he couldn't speak.

She fluffed her feathers and settled back down as if she might be staying, but then changed her mind. "Ca-coo, tuk tuk." She half flew and half ran down the sidewalk, pecking at leftover popcorn as she left.

Somewhat cheered by her visit, Imburugutu sniffed at the building and the frame of the door that rumbled. He licked it to check for salt, then magically, it lifted and revealed a whole new world. His curiosity pulled him inside. But when the metal door clattered back to the ground behind him, he realized he was shut away from the sky and the sun for the first time in his life.

At first he couldn't see anything, but after his eyes adjusted to the dim light, he saw the three giraffes on the other side of a six-foot fence. They still ignored him, so he had no other choice but to find a corner for himself.

He paced back and forth, missing the wide plains of his home. When Onosa put a large serving of alfalfa in a metal basket as tall as he was, he crunched the dry-as-dust leaves and imagined the smells of home, the feel of running with other young giraffes, the sight of lacy acacia trees, and friends who fed together in their boughs.

In the next days, Onosa came and went, busier than she'd been before. "We'll talk soon," she told him every day, even though she didn't really have time to sit and talk to Imburugutu, which made him sad. But he couldn't complain. She kept him supplied with water and alfalfa, and gave him treats of carrots, lettuce, and apples at lunch.

Between the early morning meal and dinner, a steady stream of people visited the Giraffe House. But they were unpredictable. Imburugutu felt skittish at the sound of their automatic cameras and penny whistles and loud voices. Try as he might to adapt to the variety of sounds, there was always a new one that set off his impulse to run.

Some of the people smiled. Some shouted. Some threw balls of paper; some spoke to him as if he were a baby. Some pointed at his tongue and called it black, or purple, or even green. Some tried to stroke his neck when he stood near the iron railing. However they acted, he was glad at the end of each day when the flow of people stopped.

The other giraffes still avoided him. But out of the corner of his eye, he watched those giraffes, which Onosa had called Masai. One thing he noticed about them was that they actually sat down at night, something he'd never seen a full-size giraffe do before. None of them seemed worried about *simba* and *chui* stalking them, probably because of the tall cinderblock walls that surrounded them.

One evening after dinner, he decided to give his own legs a rest. They'd grown extremely long. This would be the first time he'd sat down since he was a baby with his mother to watch over him. Slowly, Imburugutu bent his front legs, then his back ones, and painstakingly found his way to the ground. He sighed loudly with the pleasure of no weight on his legs. He rolled onto his side and released another lengthy sigh into the air. In the half-light of evening, one of the other giraffes looked over at him because he was sighing so loudly and happily. One of them was looking straight at Imburugutu for the first time.

One of them noticed me. He sighed again. *I'm not invisible. Maybe there's a place for me after all.* Even though he heard the sounds of big cats somewhere out in the night, he felt safer and more content than he had for many months. The sounds could be floating across the huge water hole he'd sailed over, or they might be as close as the other side of the Giraffe House walls. Either way, he was safe for this moment.

When the doors rumbled open the next morning, Imburugutu was already standing, again worried about lying down and being caught off his legs. Just to check, he went outside to look for signs of the big cats. There was nothing but the wire fence, the sloping wall of rocks, and an empty paddock. No sign of *simba* the lion or *chui* the leopard. Nothing moving except for the guinea hen hopping past the Giraffe House.

"Ca-coo, ca-coo, tuk tuk tuk," she said as she landed on the railing of the paddock fence. She was extra excited today, chattering faster than a gale-force wind,

sounding like the bearer of good news. Then she flut-
tered to the sidewalk to finish her rounds of the zoo.
"Ca-coo-coo-coo tuk."

Imburugutu was never sure what she said. He was
used to quiet giraffes and the businesslike oxpecker.
Even though that bird had been annoying at times,
Imburugutu missed its yellow-ringed eyes peering into
his. He missed the way it sat on his back after all its
work. But maybe the guinea hen was trying to tell him
something about his future. Maybe her arrival was a
good omen.

7

After his early morning stretch, Imburugutu went inside for breakfast, and then came the morning visiting hours. The inside of the Giraffe House had a high bridge where people could stand face to face with Imburugutu, the one Baringo giraffe, whose coat had a network of wide white lines, and with the three Masai giraffes, whose coats were spotted with patterns of dark, jagged leaves. No one, except for other giraffes, had ever looked down at Imburugutu before. No other animal had ever been taller than he was. So this noisy bridge where people dragged the heels of their shoes and leaned down into his world made him nervous and uneasy.

That morning, a class of schoolchildren was the first to clatter across the bridge.

"Hi, giraffe," one boy said, giving him a piece of popcorn when the teacher in a purple sweater wasn't watching. But the teacher seemed to have eyes in the side of her head.

"Maybe popcorn won't hurt him, but don't give him any more. See that over there?" She pointed a strong finger toward a sign: DO NOT FEED THE ANIMALS.

"He said thank you," the boy told his teacher. "Did you hear him?"

"Giraffes don't talk," the teacher answered as the boy tried to sneak another piece of popcorn to Imburugutu. "And what did I just tell you? They have their own diets, okay?" The volume of her voice was rising.

"Class, class. Quiet down and listen. Class." One of the children was trying to climb through the few inches of space below the bottom rail, tearing her dress as she did. "Get over here where you belong, Jerrilyn. You could fall and be accidentally trampled." The teacher looked as if she wanted to disappear inside her oversize purple sweater and leave her class at the zoo with the other animals.

"Even though the giraffe has that big long neck," she said, regaining her composure, "it has only seven neck bones, just like you. Feel the back of your neck. Can you find the vertebrae? Isn't that amazing? And look at that tail. Ancient Egyptians used that black hair for stringing beads and ornaments. For whisking flies, too. Modern-day Africans make bracelets and necklaces with the hair, though many countries ban

the practice. You can't get the tail without killing the giraffe."

"He's so tall, teacher," said a girl who kept bouncing up and down. "Could I ride him like a horse? Could I climb high enough?"

"In the 1600s," the teacher continued, "zoologists thought the giraffe was a cross between a camel and a leopard. Greeks named it *kamelopardalis*. Most of these scientists had never actually seen a giraffe, only heard about them, though many kings and queens had them. For many years, these regal animals were presented to emperors and kings as symbolic gifts of peace and friendship from the African countries."

A towheaded boy in blue jeans and a yellow jacket broke rank with the class and ran across the bridge. He screeched to a stop, sounding as though he had brakes of his own. In his hand, he carried a blue plastic lion from the zoo's make-your-own-animal machine. *"Rrrrgh,"* he growled at Imburugutu, making the plastic lion prance on the metal railing. *"Rrrrgh.* Here comes a predator. He's going to get you."

The screeching sounds of the boy frightened Imburugutu into pacing nervously on the concrete floor.

Onosa ran out of her office. "Stop making so much noise," she whispered so loudly it was almost a yell. "When the giraffes pace that way, they can slip and fall on the hard cement beneath the hay. Be quiet."

Imburugutu couldn't stop circling and pawing the

floor. The little boy had frightened him badly, especially the sounds from his throat that were like those of sick animals he'd heard. Then he noticed the other giraffes. They were calm and complacent and staring at him. How could they be that way while his heart was racing like a cheetah?

But one of them was watching him with what seemed like understanding. She stretched her neck over the fence that separated her from Imburugutu. She sniffed at his long, sticking-up ears, and suddenly he felt calmer. Especially calm when he looked into her eyes. So calm he didn't notice Onosa standing on the high bridge, her hand resting thoughtfully on her cheek.

"I have a surprise for you," she said when she opened Imburugutu's outside door at noontime. Then she opened the other tall rolling door and coaxed the young female giraffe outside with her usual trick of a branch of leaves. "Time for fresh air, Shining Eyes." That accomplished, she quickly pressed the button again to keep the two bulls inside.

When they met in the paddock, Imburugutu felt as if he'd always known this fine creature: her eyes, her legs, her tail. Lightning bolts zigzagged across the sides of her body and made him light-headed. The design seemed to be a mass of lace-edged leaves, their centers filled with blinding light. She was an amazing new kind of giraffe, yet she smelled familiar, like something he'd known a long time before this day.

Together, they pulled out bits of grass growing between the rocks in the walls and, when that was gone, ate one of the new shrubs the zoo's gardener had just planted outside the rail. He drove by in his beige jeep and shook his fist at the two giraffes. "How can I get anything to grow when you eat everything green?"

They paid him no mind as they drank together at the water fountain, spreading their front legs and lowering their heads to reach the water basin.

Imburugutu wished he could run and sail tails with her. Every muscle in him wanted to celebrate the happiness he felt. But if he launched into a full gallop, he'd run into a wall of rocks or a wire fence. He had grown immensely, even though he still felt like a frisky calf inside. His massive body was a stranger to him. So were his feelings when he looked at this lightning-skinned giraffe.

That afternoon, Imburugutu chewed on his alfalfa near the six-foot fence. Shining Eyes leaned over and nibbled on the stalks that stuck out of the corners of his mouth.

8

The days grew shorter and the air brisker. One morning, when Imburugutu was out for his morning exercise, whispers of snow danced across the paddock as if to say, "Be ready for me. I'm coming soon." A few flakes drifted onto his nose, and he licked one with his long gray tongue. He shivered with the new sensation of cold. He had never known it before.

When he nibbled at the grass, it broke off with a brittle snap, and his legs and tail felt as if they might snap, too. He huddled close to the building, waiting for Onosa to open his door.

"A few more days and there'll be snow on the ground," she said as Imburugutu trotted past her into shelter. "I'll give you extra alfalfa to pad your insides. You won't like it, but we'll all be staying in for a while. There's a chance that winter will be lazy this year, though, and we'll see the sun's face more than usual. Oh, that reminds me. Your name came to me last night. Sun Dancer. Do you like it?"

Imburugutu just wanted her to close the door, which she finally did, and he stood as close to Shining Eyes and as far from the cold metal door as he could. Shivering, he wished there were no fence between them.

One evening after Onosa locked her office and the Giraffe House doors and went home for the day, the older bull, whom Onosa had named Standing Eagle, walked out of the shadows to join Shining Eyes and Imburugutu. This was the first time the grandfather bull with gray bristles in his mane had paid any attention to Imburugutu. He was a friendly sort once he got used to a new situation, and he had grown tired of the younger bull, Spotted Jacket, and his fussing about how Imburugutu didn't belong.

When Spotted Jacket saw Standing Eagle being friendly with the others, he paced angrily in the moonlight that sliced through the pen's darkness from the high windows above. This was his territory. Nobody ought to forget it. Then he thrust his long neck between Shining Eyes and Imburugutu and began herding her away from the others. When she tried to escape, he stuck to her like a shadow.

Imburugutu felt his neck tensing tight, its muscles gathering power. Spotted Jacket stamped his feet and swayed his neck from side to side—*I dare you.* Imburugutu lowered his head inch by inch, not wanting to accept the challenge but feeling the impulse rise in him strongly. He saw Shining Eyes warning him with her eyes and her body movement not to fight. *No, Imburugutu.*

Before matters grew worse, Standing Eagle intervened, ambling his slow, steady, and imperial self up to Spotted Jacket. He shouldered him away from Shining Eyes and against the cinder-block wall until she was free to run back to Imburugutu.

Imburugutu licked her face until his heart stopped racing, and he was able to part from her for the night knowing Standing Eagle was there to protect her. He turned back to his lonely pen, though he twisted his neck back over his shoulder for a last look at her. He loved the sight of Shining Eyes standing there, her delicate profile highlighted by a strip of moonlight.

When Onosa returned the next morning, she decided to put all the giraffes out in the yard together. A winter storm was due, and they needed one last dose of fresh air before it arrived. They seemed to be adjusting to each other and it wouldn't hurt to let them mingle for a few minutes.

Imburugutu and Shining Eyes were the first into the yard, which seemed darker than usual. Countless clouds collided above them. When Standing Eagle and Spotted Jacket arrived, the great clouds filled the entire sky. Suddenly, thunder rolled and lightning

jumped from one end of the sky to the other. Impatient rain fell as if it had been penned up for too long. It poured out of the clouds and over the rock wall. It filled every deep groove in the ground. The yard turned into an instant water hole in a matter of seconds.

Onosa, from her place by the door, shouted, "I'll get you inside, pronto." She pushed the button that rolled the door up and down. The sound usually brought the giraffes back inside to their food. But they were confused by the sudden storm.

Even though his legs were not swaying beneath him, this storm reminded Imburugutu of the one while he was on the freighter. He watched the water racing to the lowest places in the yard and knew he should find shelter. But after the freighter, he wasn't frightened of storms. He liked water on his back, if not on his face. He liked its strong, fresh smell. It made him feel like galloping. He felt frisky and freer than he had since he'd arrived, and, for a minute, he didn't know quite where he was. He lifted his head to see if any vultures or marabou storks flew overhead.

And then he saw Spotted Jacket, the bull with the irritable temper, staring at him and lowering his head. Before Imburugutu knew what was happening, Spotted Jacket was pushing and shoving against his forequarters, circling around him, retreating, then circling again. Then he leaned heavily into Imburugutu, pressing his shoulder and flank against him to test his strength. Imburugutu had only played at this game with his calf friends a long time ago, but this was the real thing. His legs grew rigid like wooden stilts. And he spread them apart to withstand the strain of the pushing and shoving. Spotted Jacket was a much bigger bull than Imburugutu was.

Onosa pressed the door button again and again, the sound that always brought the giraffes inside. Shining Eyes and Standing Eagle backed out of the rain they didn't like, but Spotted Jacket was determined to hold Imburugutu hostage.

Curving his lowered head away from Imburugutu, he swung it at Imburugutu's neck, hitting him so hard that his forefeet lifted off the ground. The sound echoed through the rain and across to Onosa, who knew she could not stop this sparring until Spotted Jacket lost interest.

One more time, Spotted Jacket curved his head to the outside and struck Imburugutu unmercifully. When Imburugutu's feet hit the ground, they landed in slippery mud, mud that couldn't hold Imburugutu's feet steady. His hooves began sliding, farther and farther apart, sliding and sliding. Spotted Jacket retreated. Something had gone wrong. Giraffes never sparred to hurt each other. Not really. They only wanted to prove who was boss.

As Imburugutu's legs slid further, he found himself

face to face with a puddle of water. And he thought he saw something in the puddle, maybe eyes. Curious, Imburugutu looked at the puddle again. He saw pieces of giraffe in the water, distorted by the ripples.

His legs slid more and more, and now Imburugutu could get a closer look into the water. There they were. Two bright eyes watching Imburugutu. His legs slipped farther. "Am I home?" he asked. He saw two eyes, a long neck, and sticking-up ears. This reflection looked like home. It looked like his mother. It looked like the auntie cow who'd fussed after him, even like Shining Eyes. The eyes in the water were tender and filled with light.

Then time shifted again, and he saw Onosa running toward him in her raincoat and hat. "No!" she shouted as she ran across the yard. "No!"

When Imburugutu heard her, he tried to pull his legs together. But they were spread too wide. And when he tried to move, his feet slid farther apart in the mud.

"Help!" Onosa shouted as she tried to push one leg back under Imburugutu. "Somebody! Help! Come on, Sun Dancer," she pleaded. "Help me. Help me get you back on your feet."

But Imburugutu couldn't help Onosa or himself. He had no strength to pull himself back to a standing position.

"I've got to phone for help." Onosa raced away.

Imburugutu's neck hurt when he was down like this but, out of instinct, he held it high. He wished he could roll over, out of this awkward position, but he couldn't move in any way.

Running and splashing through the mud, Onosa returned with a blanket for Imburugutu. She spread it over his back and massaged his neck.

People came from everywhere. Children in their yellow rain slickers and black galoshes. School teachers with plastic-covered clipboards. Grandmothers with their umbrellas. Workers with plastic capes covering their green uniforms. Trucks. Forklifts. Even the guinea hen hopped up on the railing. She shifted her weight from leg to leg, rocking nervously.

The crowd grew while a confusion of animal keepers shouted back and forth to each other.

"No ropes. Trauma to his neck. No pulleys." First came the small trucks with their drivers puzzling what to do. Then the tow trucks with winches and harnesses. A small battalion of working machines crawled over the sidewalks of the zoo, destination Giraffe House, operation to help the giraffe stand again, to rescue the tall, graceful, dignified animal.

"Nothing's big enough," Onosa shouted. "We need a machine bigger than he is."

"There's a crane digging a sewer line on the street west of the zoo," the rhino keeper said.

"Somebody go get it."

"Does that mean me?" the rhino keeper asked.

"Somebody has to go."

Imburugutu felt his heart roaring like *simba* inside his chest. He felt the helplessness of his legs and the awkwardness of his body stretched over the ground. He was glad for the eyes he'd seen all through his life—the eyes in the water, eyes of friends, and eyes in the clouds at sunset. The eyes that had always protected and stayed with him. And he was glad that the rain was thinning to a drizzle, to a mist that didn't sting his face.

Two large men, the manager of concessions and the camel keeper, climbed out of a truck and ran to either side of Imburugutu, carefully pushing his legs back together. Since his spindly legs would slide apart again if they weren't propped, the men leaned against them to keep them from splitting again. They stood for long minutes that slowly ticked away. An awkward silence settled over the crowd of onlookers.

It seemed hours until they heard the sound of a large, bulky crane lumbering along the sidewalk, its metal treads crunching the concrete. "Thank God," the camel keeper said. "Can you feel how this animal's legs are trembling?"

"Open the gate again." Onosa tossed a ring of keys across the yard to someone she didn't even know and kept stroking Imburugutu's side to reassure him.

The sound of grinding gears cut through the revived

noise of the crowd. The crane rumbled into the paddock with a large harness dangling from its boom.

"Hurry," Onosa yelled to the crane operator.

The crane operator lowered the harness.

"You get on this side," Onosa ordered the rhino keeper. "We've got to slide these straps underneath him without frightening him too much."

All the while Onosa rubbed and patted Imburugutu. "Beautiful Sun Dancer. We'll help you. Hang on." She checked the blanket to make sure it still covered his back. "It's okay. I'm with you." Her hands soothed him.

Two men hooked the straps under Imburugutu's chest, in between his front and back legs. They connected them to the hook block, and signaled the crane operator to raise the boom.

"We'll get him up with this," one of them shouted. "We're going to get him on his feet."

"They're getting him on his feet." The news traveled out of the yard and into the crowd. "Up on his legs!" All the people cheered for the long-necked, sticking-up-ears giraffe. He would soon be as he had been. Tall, gentle. Standing on his own legs.

The crane dipped its long neck when it lifted Imburugutu off the ground. His legs bent underneath him. Then it slowly lifted him higher until his four limp legs drew together, splattered with mud. Everyone held their breath as the crane finally lifted him off the ground and his four legs dangled above the muddy flat. But when the boom lowered him to a drier place where he could stand once again, his legs folded like tissue paper.

"Lower him to his side," Onosa ordered. "His heart's beating as fast as a running deer's." She signaled the crane operator to lower Imburugutu to the ground, but then shouted, "Wait a minute!"

Imburugutu looked around, and then he saw that Shining Eyes had come out of the cinder-block building. She walked to his side, delicately nuzzled his neck, then gazed at him with eyes much like those he'd seen in the rain puddle.

He heard Shining Eyes talking in her own way to the other giraffes, who'd followed behind. Shining Eyes, Standing Eagle, Spotted Jacket, and Imburugutu all looked up at the clouds, now breaking apart and letting through great shafts of sunlight. It was Imburugutu's turn to go back to the earth and toward new life.

And though Imburugutu was still in the crane's harness, he was already sailing across the wide plains, the wind carrying his tail as he floated toward the whistling thorn whose fragrance and whose tender leaves pleased him and invited him back home again.

Afterword

Today, wild animals are rarely imported. Most zoos trade with other zoos and breed their animals in captivity. Transporting giraffes to and from locations, however, is still very hazardous because of their great height.

The language used by Imburugutu in Kenya is Swahili, and his story is based on an incident involving a real giraffe named Vincent at the Marwell Zoological Park in Colden Common, Winchester, Hampshire, England. Circumstances leading up to and surrounding the final scene are, for the most part, imagined.